Contents

Sounds in this book

a-e (cave)   ay (today)   c (city)   e (secrets)
ea (reach)   ew (new)   i-e (mine)   o-e (bone)
oi (coins)   ou (ground, you)   ue (blue)
wh (what)

Under the ground

Look down at the ground. What do you think is underneath you?

Secret rooms?

A hidden cave?

Lots of pipes?

An old mine?

A chest full of gold coins!

A nice bone!

Let's take a look under the ground. There is lots to see down there!

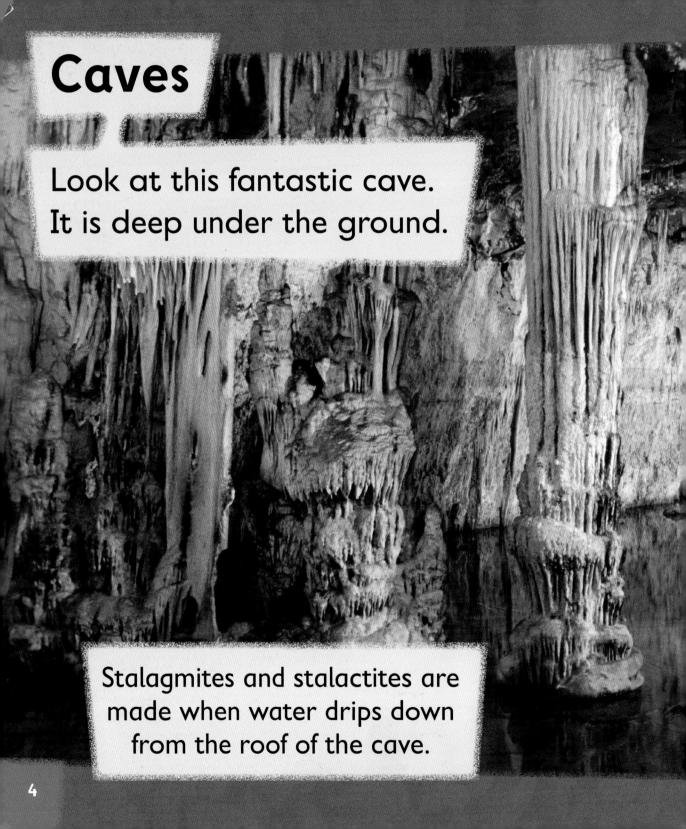

Caves

Look at this fantastic cave.
It is deep under the ground.

Stalagmites and stalactites are
made when water drips down
from the roof of the cave.

4

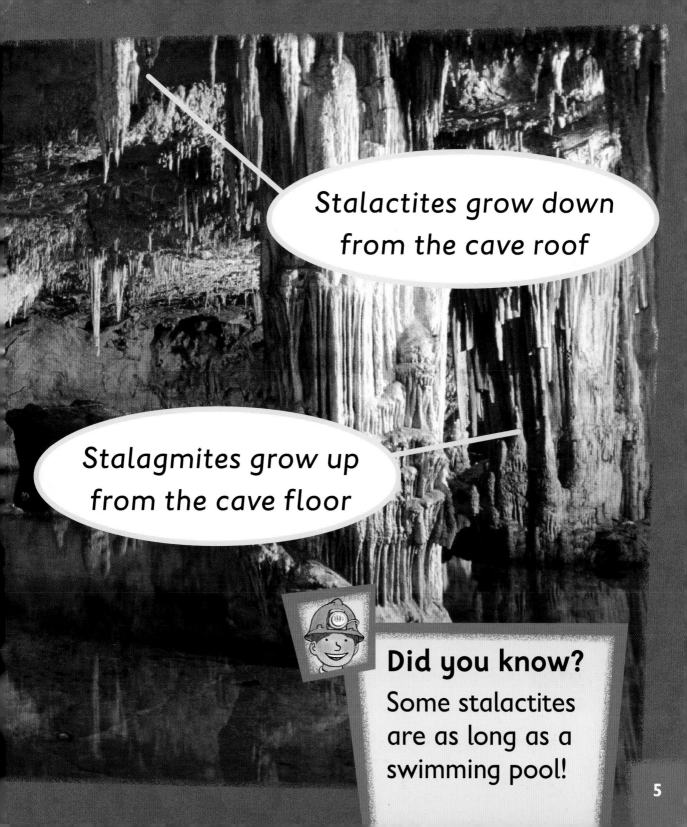

This man is exploring an underground cave.

He has to squeeze down holes to reach the cave.

That hole looks very small!

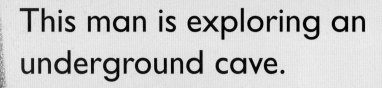

hard hat

torch

What is different about this cave?

It's under the sea!

You need to be a good
diver to explore these caves.

Mines

Coal, tin and even gold can come from under the ground. It is very hard to dig for coal.

These are coal miners from the past.

lantern

pickaxe

Salt can also be found under the ground.

This stunning chapel is in a salt mine in Poland. Look closely. What do you think it is made of?

salt statue

salt wall

salt light

All of it is made from salt!

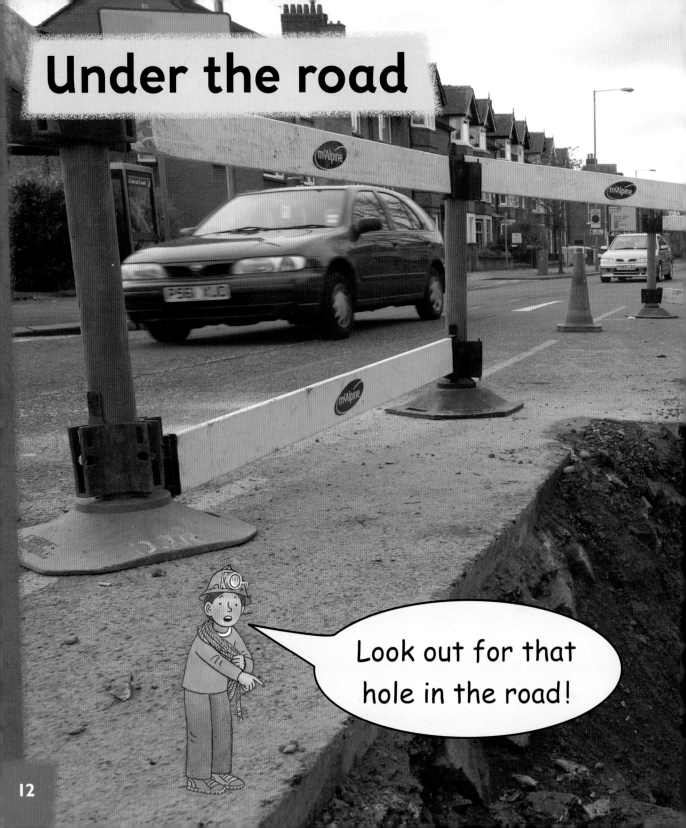

Under the road

Look out for that hole in the road!

The pipes carry things like gas and electricity.

Transport

Here comes an underground train. Jump on! You could travel deep under a big city.

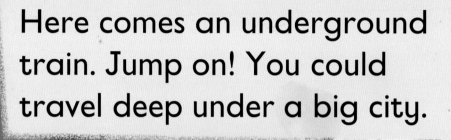

There are underground railways in lots of cities.

This one is in Canada.

Houses

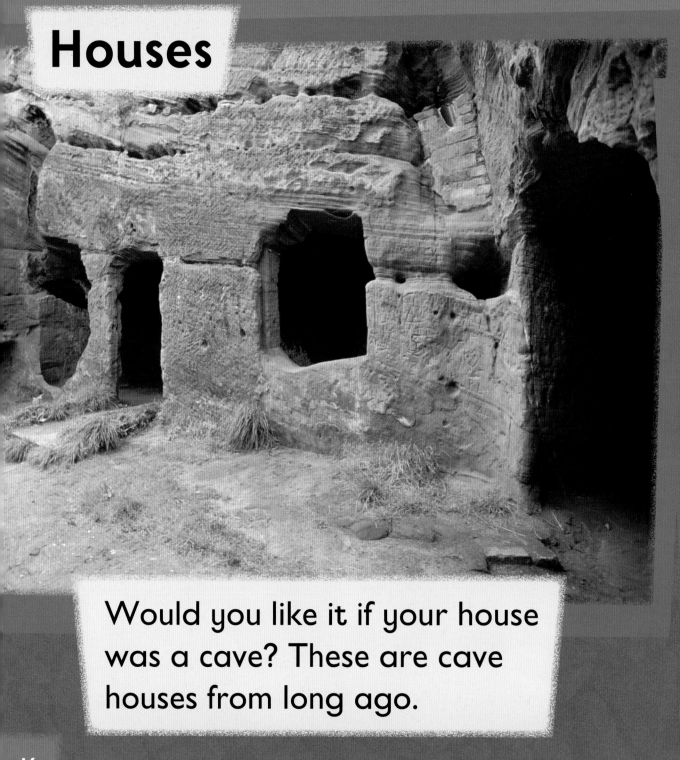

Would you like it if your house was a cave? These are cave houses from long ago.

These cave houses are over 700 years old!

Did you know?
There are still cave houses today.

Look at this new house.
It is under a hill.

The windows give the house
light, and the hill helps to
keep the heat in.

Underground secrets

Let's explore some secret underground places. Look at all those bones!

They are in a room under a church.

This room is deep under the ground. It was a secret telephone room.

Did you know?

This room is in Dover. There are three miles of secret tunnels in Dover too!

21

Underground places to visit in the UK

Cheddar Cave and Gorge

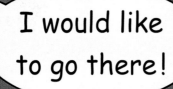

I would like to go there!

Kent's Cavern

Blue John Mine

Grimes Graves

Index